Contents

The Mum-Manager

by

Suzi Cresswell

Illustrated by Vince Reid

First Published
April 08 in Great Britain by

PUBLISHING

© **Suzi Cresswell 2008**

ISBN-10: 1-905637-45-4
ISBN-13: 978-1-905637-45-4

Educational Printing Services Limited
Albion Mill, Water Street, Great Harwood, Blackburn BB6 7QR
Telephone: (01254) 882080   Fax: (01254) 882010
E-mail: enquiries@eprint.co.uk   Website: www.eprint.co.uk

Chapter 1
A Volunteer

'So do I have a volunteer?' said the man in the tracksuit.

Several parents looked at the ground as if it had suddenly become fascinating. Toby saw Leroy nudge his dad, who shook his head.

'Come on, I need a name on this form today or the team folds!' The man in the tracksuit, who was called Dave, looked round at the crowd of parents and players.

'Without a name they'll be no training, no matches, nothing. I can't manage the boys from Scotland now can I? Come on someone please?'

SILENCE.

Toby saw Leroy frown. Jacko looked near to tears. Lofty the goalie banged his gloves together and smiled nervously.

'Compton Colts have had a brilliant season. They were runners up in the league, they're improving all the time. It would be a crime if it all has to end.'

Dave was starting to get angry now.

Jacko looked at his dad. Toby and the boys had talked about Dave leaving. Everyone had been upset but Jacko had said, 'My dad will take over. He loves footy.'

Jacko's dad blushed and said, 'You know I'd love to. But with the new job and the baby I won't have time.'

Jacko did start to cry then. His eyes went red and huge tears rolled down his cheeks.

That's it, thought Toby, *there's no-one else. Compton Colts will have to disband.* He had been sure that Jacko's dad would take over as manager. That's what the team had been expecting when they heard that Dave was moving to Scotland. Then he heard a whisper. Mum was mouthing something to Rose, Leroy's mum. There it was again. It was Mum. Then she put her hand up like she was in school.

'I'll do it,' she said softly, 'I'll manage the Colts. I don't know anything about football but how difficult can it be?'

'And I'll help Sharon,' said Leroy's mum, Rose.

Toby stared at his mum, stunned. *She was right about one thing*, he thought, *she knew nothing, absolutely zilch, zero, minus nothing about football. OK, she came to the matches, collected money for the ref' and*

4

washed the kit, but managing them? No chance!

'Mum . . . are you sure?' Toby hissed, 'You don't know a corner from a throw in, or a goal kick from a penalty kick!'

'Dave's right, someone has to do it. And we can learn, can't we Rose?' said Sharon. Rose ran over. They were laughing and hugging each other.

'Can I be the one who runs on with the bag?' asked Rose, 'I've always wanted to do that!'

Leroy rolled his eyes heavenward and pulled a face. Toby knew he was embarrassed too.

'Doesn't look like we have a choice,' whispered Toby to Leroy, 'No-one else volunteered.'

'I know . . . rubbish though, isn't it?'

'Well thank you Sharon and Rose. I think that's really great of you,' said Dave. He came over and started shaking their hands but Sharon hugged him instead.

'Aren't you proud of your mums boys?' he added when Sharon released him.

Toby looked at Leroy. Their eyes widened and both tried not to pull faces.

'Yeah,' stammered Toby, ' 'course.'

Leroy nodded.

'Oh bless!' said Sharon and gave him a sticky, lipstick kiss.

'Geroff . . . ,' muttered Toby, wiping his cheek. *Proud?* he thought, *Dave must be mad, it was a disaster!*

Chapter Two
First Training Session

'Hang forward, loose and floppy like a ragdoll!' shouted Sharon.

Jacko and Lofty nudged one another and giggled.

Sharon walked over to them and placed a hand on each of their backs, 'That's it boys. Feel that lovely stretch.'

'Now into the down facing dog,' said Sharon, walking her feet back, 'That's it Lofty.'

'Woof,' said Leroy to Toby, laughing.

Sharon shot them a warning glance. 'Back into the hang forward.'

'Am I still being a dog?' asked Jacko.

Sharon clapped her hands. 'Up you come. Great work everyone, thank you so much.'

Toby groaned, 'But Mum we haven't played any football!'

It was true. Training had started with a warm up dance. Rose had stood in the front doing a complicated routine to 'Three Lions'. She said it would inspire them. She had even changed the words a bit so that the chorus went,

    'Three Lions on the shirt,
    Compton Colts still breathing,
    Sharon and Rose in charge,
    Never stopped them dreaming.'

It was a bit of a laugh when everyone went wrong. Lofty's dancing had been especially terrible.

Then there had been a 'chat'. More like an interrogation, thought Toby. Sharon and Rose had made them sit round in a circle and talk to the person on their right. Then they'd had to tell everyone else what was said. Mum kept interrupting, saying things like, 'So how is your mum, Jacko? Is the baby still waking up in the night?'

She seemed to have a list of questions for everyone. Toby thought she was the nosiest person he knew. *Why did she need to know about Leroy's grandma's lumbago,* he thought, or *whether Lofty enjoyed his holiday? It wasn't going to help them as a football team!*

Then there was lots of stretching.

Sharon was a yoga teacher when she wasn't hairdressing. How was doing the down

facing dog and dancing going to help The Colts ?
Toby felt himself getting very cross.

'Mu-um! When are we going to do any
footy?' he repeated.

Sharon grinned. 'Yes Tobias. I 'm coming
to that.'

'Oooh Tobias,' teased Jacko.

Toby reddened. Nobody ever called him
Tobias. Everyone called him Toby. His
teachers, his friends, everyone except Mum.
Now he would never hear anything else.

'OK. Just do some passing practice or
something. Whatever you normally do . . . ,'
said Sharon vaguely. The boys looked a bit
unsure but got a ball each and began passing
in pairs.

Sharon and Rose walked round the boys
shouting encouragement.

'Oh super kick,' said Sharon and ruffled Lofty's hair, 'bless.'

'Tell me if you need any spray or icepacks!' insisted Rose. She looked longingly at her pink holdall which contained the first aid kit.

Leroy passed to Toby. They both grimaced.

'Come back Dave, all is forgiven,' muttered Toby.

'I liked it when he yelled at us,' said Leroy.

'Me too, I liked being called 'twitness' and 'numbskull',' added Toby.

'Or when he just said 'Not bad lad' when you scored a hat trick!' said Leroy.

'Our mums, they're over the top aren't they?' said Toby.

After a few minutes it was time to stop.

'I'll see you all at the barbecue on Sunday,' said Sharon. She and Rose had organized a 'Getting-to-know-you Barbecue' for all the players and parents. Toby was dreading it.

'And before you go, I've got something to show you!' said Sharon.

The boys gathered round as Rose struggled from the car with a big cardboard box.

'It's our new strip,' said Sharon excitedly. 'My boss from the salon offered to sponsor us.'

She rummaged round and pulled out a pale yellow shirt, covered in big blue spots. Across the front was written, 'Curl Up and Dye.'

'Gorgeous isn't it?'

Toby stared, stupefied. 'Curl Up and Dye,' he muttered, 'that's exactly what I feel like doing.'

Chapter Three
Toby's Plan

'If she thinks I'm wearing that, she's got another think coming!' complained Toby after the training.

'The shirts aren't that bad,' said Leroy, 'at least they're not pink and frilly.'

'I don't think I can stand Mum as a manager,' said Toby, 'there's got to be someone else.'

'Tough luck Tobias,' joked Leroy.

Toby swung his kit bag at him and they started play fighting.

'Tobias?' shouted someone. It was Sharon. 'Say sorry to Leroy!'

'It's alright Sharon, we're only messing,' explained Leroy. He grinned and Toby laughed.

'How do you think training went?' asked Sharon.

Both boys looked at one another. 'Er . . . a bit more footy next time perhaps?' said Toby.

'And less dancing and bending,' added Leroy.

Sharon nodded. 'You two could have

taken the yoga a bit more seriously, especially the down facing dog.'

'Sorry Sharon,' said Leroy, 'it's just that....' He began laughing and barking, 'woof woof, woof woof.'

Sharon grinned, 'Bless,' she said.

'I'm just going to Leroy's to see his new game,' said Toby.

'Don't be long, you've got homework,' warned his mum.

🏆 🏆 🏆

At Leroy's, Toby grabbed a piece of paper and began writing . He wrote, 'How to get a new manager' and underlined it. *We have to do something*, he told himself.

'What about the new boy at school?' he said. 'Ginger. Do you think we can get him to join the team? Maybe then his dad can manage us?'

'It's worth a try,' replied Leroy, 'he told me a footy joke the other day, so he must like football.'

'And we could advertise. Put a card in the shop or something?' Toby knew that Mum did that when she wanted to sell his old swing.

Leroy was flicking through Toby's 'Striker' magazine which had footy quizzes, letters and articles about players in it.

Toby leaned over to look at it. A headline leapt out:

'Do you want to win coaching

**sessions from Donchester Legend
Matty Fox?'**

He pointed to it and he and Leroy read
the article.

'You have to write, saying why your
team needs help,' said Toby.

'What could we put?' asked Leroy.

'Easy. Just tell them about the two mad mothers managing us, who know nothing about football. And about the rubbish strip, that's enough surely.'

'But won't Sharon and Rose be upset?' said Leroy.

'They won't need to know unless we win. Look, you do the advert for the shop. I'll do the letter and ask Ginger to the barbecue.'

Leroy was hesitant, 'Well I like Sharon. But my mum is just so embarrassing. All that dancing tonight and changing the words to Three Lions. She's got loads more dances planned. I don't think I can stand it.'

'With my mum's yoga and Rose's dances, we'll never get to do any training,' added Toby. 'We'll end up the joke of the league.'

Leroy sighed, 'You're right.'

Toby looked at his list. It said:

•	**Ask Ginger's dad**
•	**Put advert in shop**
•	**Write to The Striker**

'That's three things to try,' pointed out
Toby. 'One of them should do the trick.'

Chapter 4
The 'Getting-to-know-you' Barbecue

Ginger was sitting on the bench with his dad. Unfortunately Ginger had also brought his twin sister. She was red haired too and kept flicking her pony tail. Her name was Sky and she looked bored. *Nobody asked her to come,* thought Toby.

'Why was the mummy no good at football?' asked Ginger.

'Dunno,' said Toby.

'Because she was too wrapped up in herself.' Ginger giggled helplessly.

'I think girls can play football just as well as boys!' said Sky.

'Huh, I don't know any,' Toby replied crossly.

Sky shrugged and walked off, tossing her ponytail.

'Do you want to join the team?' Toby asked Ginger later, as they ate burgers. 'Only when Dave left he took Tom, the striker, so we are short of one player.'

Ginger looked thrilled. As if he couldn't believe his luck.

'Me, really? I'd love to!'

Leroy caught his eye and frowned. Of course Toby didn't really know if Ginger was any good. *He'd just started the school last week. He does look a bit small,* thought Toby. *A bit knock kneed. Still lots of good players are small,* he told himself.

Toby decided to talk to Ginger's dad. 'Do you like football?'

'Oh yes, always supported Donchester, me.'

'Did you play when you were younger?' asked Toby. He really wanted a manager who used to play football a lot and knew all the rules.

Ginger's dad smiled sadly. 'Couldn't play for toffee, me. I get terrible asthma. So does Ginger. It's Sky who's the sporty one. You should ask her to play for you. '

Toby began to realize that the plan to get Ginger and his dad involved in the team was not a good one. He sighed with disappointment. Then he really thought about what Ginger's dad had said. *No way do we need a girl,* he thought, *especially not River or Stream or whatever she was called.*

Later Leroy and Jacko were taking shots at Lofty in Toby's goal in the garden. In between shots, Toby noticed that Jacko was chatting to Sky.

'Can I have a go?' she asked. Toby watched. *Flippin' cheek, she'll be rubbish,* he thought to himself, *all girls are.*

Sky did about twenty skilful keep ups. Then she tossed the ball up high and trapped it on her back.

Toby stood by open mouthed. He'd been trying to learn that trick for ages and still

hadn't mastered it. 'Come on,' she said to Jacko, 'try and get the ball off me.'

Jacko was a good tackler but Sky was far too fast for him. She dodged this way and that, swerving round Jacko as if he had two left feet. Then she checked and belted the ball at the goal. Lofty got a finger to it but it fizzed over and went in the top corner. Even in his present mood Toby could see that she was good. Sharon had been watching, plate of burgers in hand.

'Sky, I think you have to be my first proper signing. What do you say?' Sharon rushed over and gave Sky a great big hug. 'Just in time for our first friendly next week.'

Toby glared at Leroy, 'That's all we need,' he hissed, 'a flippin' girl.'

'Our new shirts will really suit your colouring Sky,' Sharon said, stroking her red pony tail.

Rose had rushed over to join them. 'I bet you're a great little dancer,' she said.

Toby put his head in his hands and let out a long groan.

Chapter 5
A Reply

Toby was bowed but not defeated. He realized that Ginger's dad wouldn't be any better than Sharon as a manager. There's still the advert that Leroy put in the shop and the letter to The Striker, he told himself. He had spent ages writing it and in the end he was pleased with his effort. It read,

Dear Striker,
    My team Compton Colts is in real trouble.

Our manager has left leaving no-one in charge. My mum Sharon, and her friend Rose are trying to look after things but it's a disaster. All we do is dance and stretches, no proper training at all! We have a terrible new strip and to cap it all Mum has just signed a girl. The new season starts in 2 weeks. We really desperately need Matty Fox to come and give us some help.

From Toby.

Please pick us, he thought as he put the letter in his pocket to post on his way to Leroy's. As he walked along, Toby imagined The Colts winning The Striker's competition and meeting Matty Fox. Matty might even decide to take over as manager himself. *Think of what he could teach us*, thought Toby, *we'd probably win the league and the cup with help like that.* Toby imagined holding a cup up high and a team photo appearing in the local paper.

'Hi,' shouted a voice behind him.

Toby turned. *Oh no*, he thought, *it's Sky and Ginger*.

Sky was holding a football. 'We're going for a kick about in the park. Want to come?'

Ginger bounded over.

'Why did the manager want the pitch flooded?' asked Ginger.

Toby paused. 'Dunno,' he mumbled.

'So he could bring on his subs,' said Ginger, laughing loudly. 'Sure you can't come?'

Toby shook his head, 'I've got to go out,' he lied.

'Suit yourself Tobias. I'd better get on and practise, I don't want to let the team down on Sunday,' said Sky.

Toby stared after them. *Stupid idiot,* he thought, *just who does she think she is, calling me Tobias and joining a boy's team?* He put his hands in his pocket and marched along the road, kicking the kerb. Now they were stuck with Sky and Ginger because Sharon had signed both of them. *I don't even think Ginger's any good,* thought Toby, but Sharon had said, 'He's so excited, bless him, we'll have to give him a go.'

Toby marched along to Leroy's getting crosser and crosser. *I wish I'd never asked Ginger to join*, he thought, *all he does is tell jokes and now we've got his rotten sister too.*

♛ ♛ ♛

'Have you had any replies to the advert?' asked Toby when he got to Leroy's.

Leroy looked a bit puzzled.

'Well I put the notice in the shop asking for a coach. I didn't know how to write manager. Two people have phoned so far.'

'What did they say?' asked Toby excitedly.

Leroy shook his head. 'That's just it. One said something about being nearly new and blue. The other one asked if I wanted a foot stool or something.'

Toby tried to make sense of this. Then he remembered that Leroy wasn't the best speller. 'What did you write exactly?' he asked.

Leroy showed him a card. On it he had written the advert. 'I didn't use this one because the writing was a bit small. I copied it out the same but bigger.'

Toby looked at it. He read:
Footy couch wanted.
Phone 08796 787878.

Toby felt like screaming. 'Coach, not couch, you twitness!' he shouted.

'Numbskull,' added Leroy, grinning.

Just then the phone went. Toby answered it.

'I've got a lovely leather couch and I could throw in a couple of armchairs too?' said a man's voice. 'Hardly used 'cos the missus never liked them.'

'No thanks,' replied Toby, his voice cracking as he tried not to laugh. 'We're sorted now thanks.'

Toby put the phone down and they both laughed and laughed.

'First we end up with a girl in the team,' said Toby, suddenly serious, 'and then someone offers you a nearly new couch and me a leather one with chairs thrown in!'

'We could start up a sofa and chair shop,' said Leroy with a grin.

'But the season starts soon,' Toby reminded him, 'the letter to The Striker is our last hope!'

Chapter 6
First Friendly

It was ten minutes into the first half. Things weren't going too badly. The match was a friendly against Longton Lions. The Colts had played them last season. Even the new strip didn't look that bad, thought Toby, although he still hated the spots and the logo. Rose had brought a tape player and tried to get them dancing to 'Three Lions' at the start. Toby and Leroy had joined in half heartedly but the rest of the team had loved it.

The other team had watched on with
interest and some of them had joined in.

'Superb for warming up,' Rose had told
the other team, 'and for keeping fit. Wait
till you see The Colts in action.'

Sharon was dressed in a purple
tracksuit with new silver trainers. Rose was
sitting in a folding deckchair. She had the
pink bag in her hand and kept saying, 'As

soon as anyone's injured I'll run on!'

It was nil-nil. Sky was on and so far even Toby had to admit she had played OK. Ginger was sub and was telling jokes to anyone who'd listen.

'When is a footballer like a baby?' he asked.

Toby wished Mum wasn't quite so nice. She kept calling out, 'Super', 'Fabulous' and 'Brilliant'. Not for the first time Toby missed Dave.

When Lofty made a good save, just before the interval, Sharon blew him a kiss and shouted, 'Great isn't he Rose? Bless him!'

Toby had pulled his shirt over his head to hide his face.

'I can't stand it,' he muttered to Leroy, 'Mum is driving me nuts.'

The whistle blew for half time. Sharon had got them all matching drinks bottles with their names on and she was passing round orange slices. Rose followed her handing out wipes so they could wipe any sticky fingers.

Ginger rushed up to finish the joke, 'When he dribbles,' he said laughing.

Sky glared at her brother. *He's really starting to get on my nerves*, thought Toby.

'Well done Colts. You are being super. Just great!' said Sharon.

'Good game so far,' added Rose. 'Don't forget if anyone gets a knock, I'm ready with the bag.'

She opened it and checked the sprays, bandages and ice packs.

'Sky you are fitting in brilliantly,' said Sharon, 'fabulous.' She gave her a hug and Toby groaned when he heard Mum say, 'We girls must stick together.'

In the second half things started to go

wrong. The number 9 from the other side was heard snapping at Jacko, 'You look a right sight in those spotty shirts. S'pose your lady manager chose those for you.'

Jacko had always had a bit of a short fuse and he started to push the other player. The ref' stopped the match to calm the boys down. Sharon intervened.

'Look ref', it was only a teensy little push. Could you overlook it just for me?' Amazingly the ref' blushed and agreed. But the peace didn't last long. The number 9 started chanting, 'It's one in the eye for 'Curl up and Dye'.'

'Now hang on,' shouted Jacko, squaring up to the other boy. That's when the number 9 gave Jacko an almighty shove and he fell, spread eagled on the floor. The ref' went over to inspect the damage just as Rose rushed off her deckchair and sprinted over.

Somehow, Toby was never quite sure how, but Rose, tripped and went flying through the air, flattening the ref' and Jacko.

'Rose, Jacko, ref'!' yelled Sharon. She took one look at the mess of limbs and fished out her phone and called an ambulance.

They came in a few minutes. It took nearly half an hour for Rose, the ref' and Jacko to be untangled. Rose's earring had got caught in the ref's whistle string and in Jacko's hair. Rose had sprayed the deep heat muscle spray everywhere including in the ref's eyes. All three were moaning.

'They may have head injuries,' said the paramedic. 'They'll have to stay in hospital overnight.'

Toby put his head in his hands. What a first match! Just over half way through and it had to be abandoned. The whole thing was a nightmare. He glanced at his mum who looked pale and shaken. If only I could win the coaching sessions from The Striker, everything would be OK, Toby told himself.

Chapter 7
No Reply from The Striker

For the last few days Toby had hung around trying to catch the post.

In the afternoon a handwritten note arrived addressed to Toby. He studied the writing, feeling puzzled. Perhaps it's from Jacko or Lofty. *A birthday invitation or something*, he thought.

The note said:

Dear Toby,

We were sorry to hear about the troubles at Compton Colts. It's always difficult when a team has a new manager. We were impressed with your letter and have an idea about how to help you. Meet us at 7pm in the park.

From some friends

What the heck? thought Toby, *this is like something out of a spy movie.*

Toby rushed round to show Leroy.

'Who's it from?' asked Leroy, 'It can't be The Striker because look . . . '

Leroy showed Toby the new copy of The Striker. At the front the editor had written a special note to readers. It said:

**'Because of the huge response
to our competition for coaching
sessions with Matty Fox, it will be
several months before we decide on
a winner. Sorry teams, but it's the
only fair way.'**

'I dunno. But you're coming with me,'
said Toby.

'Let's go in disguise, just in case it's a
joke,' said Leroy, 'and then we can slip away.'

At 7 o'clock sharp Toby and Leroy
walked to the park. Both were wearing
baseball hats and sunglasses. The first
people Toby saw were Sky and Ginger.

'Those two follow me around,' Toby
complained.

To his amazement Sky came over.

'So much for being in disguise,' hissed

Toby. Leroy took off his glasses.

'You got the note then?' she said.

'It was from you? What do you want?' said Toby, a little rudely.

Ginger came over too. 'You dropped your letter to The Striker,' explained Ginger, 'I'm sorry but we opened it and that's how we found out what you thought about The Colts and how you wanted help from Matty Fox.'

'Oh,' said Toby. He knew he had complained about Sky in the letter. He felt himself blushing.

'The thing is, we have an idea that might help. And someone for you to meet,' said Sky. She took them over to a woman sitting on the bench.

'This is our mum,' said Sky. 'She works for T.V.'

Toby glanced at the small, blonde haired woman. She was wearing a black trouser suit and was tapping away on a small laptop. She paused to talk into a slim, black, flip phone.

'Yes, they're here now. I'll run it past

them and get back to you.'

She turned and looked them up and down.

She looks like Sky, thought Toby, *only scarier.*

'Hello. Tobias and Leroy isn't it? I'm Tessa. Sky and Ginger have told me lots about you and The Colts. They have an idea, it might just work. But first I have to know if you think Sharon and Rose have any chance of learning to manage the team?'

Toby looked at Leroy. He thought hard. Somehow Toby knew this was important. He thought about his mum trying her best, and about Rose and her dances. 'I think they could. They were brave enough to take on the job when no-one else would.'

Leroy nodded, 'My mum gets on my nerves, Sharon gets on his nerves but we could cope if they knew even a tiny bit about football.'

Tessa nodded. 'Boys,' she smiled, 'listen to Sky's idea. It just might work.'

Chapter 8
A Visitor

On Thursday at 5.50 the team was assembled on the training ground. Rose and Jacko were both out of hospital. Rose was subdued and wore sunglasses.

'It's 'cos she's got a black eye,' said Leroy.

Sharon was dressed in a blue and lilac tracksuit. She looked jumpy and kept checking her watch.

At six o' clock exactly a dark car drew up and someone got out. A figure in a baseball cap and glasses came out of the car. Toby grinned. It had to be Matty Fox.

The man walked up to Mum and said, 'I'm looking for Tobias.'

Toby shuddered. Everyone had started calling him Tobias, but never mind. He wasn't going to hold it against Matty Fox of all people.

'I'm Toby,' he said a little loudly, 'over here.'

The man approached and took off the baseball cap and glasses. It was Matty.

The team gasped. Jacko rushed to find something for Matty to sign. Lofty launched into 'Three Lions' with Rose, who suddenly seemed back to her old self.

Matty put up his hand, 'I've heard about the dancing,' he said, 'and I can't wait to see the yoga.'

Matty cleared his throat. Toby could see everyone watching him. *It really is him,* he thought, *here on our field.*

'Hi Guys, you may know who I am,' he said. Everyone laughed. *You'd need to be a visiting alien not to have heard of Matty,* thought Toby.

'A little bird told me you might need a bit of extra coaching. Is that right?'

Toby looked anxiously over at Mum. She didn't seem surprised. She kept patting her hair and smiling.

'So let's get training. You must be Sharon, come and be my assistant,' said Matty smoothly.' You can show me your yoga routine later.'

Before long Matty had them practising passing drills. He showed them how to control the ball. He showed them how to swerve and twist and how to wrong foot opponents. The team was awestruck. He even seemed to teach Ginger how to pass the ball better.

'It's just like telling jokes Ginger,' said Matty, 'it's all in the delivery.'

'Isn't he brill'? mouthed Leroy.

'Magic,' agreed Toby.

Then they had a little game. Matty made some suggestions about where players should play and wrote notes for Sharon.

Rose perked up and kept saying things like, 'Wait until you see the other dance moves we've got,' and 'I can make up the Matty Fox move if you like.'

Toby and Leroy watched with interest. Matty didn't seem annoyed. He seemed to be enjoying himself, laughing and joking with their mums.

'You've got some great players,' commented Matty, 'Sky is a very good first signing too. Congratulations!'

At the end Matty said, 'I know you've got your first match on Sunday. I'll come along and support you.'

After he'd gone they all seemed to float home on a cloud. Even Sharon seemed star-struck.

'Wasn't he handsome?' she kept saying

to Rose. 'So friendly and polite.'

'I reckon he's a real, cool guy,' agreed Rose.

'How did he know about us?' asked Jacko, 'I mean someone must have told him about The Colts, but who?'

'Yeah,' said Lofty, 'he seemed to know all our names, all about my great dance moves, even . . . '

Toby looked at Leroy. *We can't say,* thought Toby, *we promised we'd keep quiet until tonight.* Toby could see Sky and Ginger walking over. Sky was smiling.

'Yes, how did Matty know about my little bro's rubbish jokes?' she asked.

'Watch the local news tonight,' said Toby, 'seven o' clock.'

Chapter 9
On T.V.

'Shhh,' said Sharon, 'we're on next.'

They were all gathered around at Toby's, eyes glued to the T.V. screen. After he had told Lofty and the others to watch the news most of the team decided to watch it together. Sharon had rung round the parents and several had come over.

'What are we waiting for?' asked Jacko

impatiently as The News dragged on. Toby hoped that everything had gone to plan. He was just beginning to despair when Leroy gave him a nudge.

'And now for a football team with a difference,' said the newsreader, 'We sent our reporter to watch a typical training session with Compton Colts.'

Sharon flashed onto the screen saying, 'Feel that lovely stretch.'

Then the camera switched to Rose and Sharon sitting in a circle with the team chatting.

'Sharon isn't your usual junior football manager,' said Tessa. 'In fact she doesn't know much about football and has never played. But Sharon teaches yoga and her assistant Rose, likes dancing.'

There was Rose on T.V., running through the dance to 'Three Lions'.

'Sharon has a very special reason for signing up as manager for the Colts,' explained Tessa.

'No one else would do it,' said Sharon, 'It was either me or the team folded.'

The camera swung over to Rose, 'We couldn't let that happen. Our Leroy and Toby would have been heartbroken.' Rose was seen checking the pink holdall and rolling up a few bandages.

Sharon and Rose were staring at the screen.

'We're famous,' said Rose.

'I'm so glad I did our hair,' said Sharon. 'Yours looks great.'

Tessa was on the screen now, looking very professional and confident.

'We at News Roundup think that Sharon is very brave and wanted to help out. So because her knowledge of football is a little, er, non existent, we decided to arrange for The Colts and 'The Mum Manager' to have training sessions with Matty Fox, the Donchester legend. Over the next few weeks we'll be following their progress.'

Then there was a short interview with Matty, which Toby thought must have been filmed earlier in the day.

'I'm always up for a challenge,' said Matty, smiling, 'and I liked the sound of The Mum Manager and her assistant. Our first training session is tonight and then I'll be able to see what Sharon and Rose need to work on.'

The Colts started cheering. Toby and Leroy grinned at one another.

'I wonder what he thinks now he's met

us?' asked Jacko.

'He thinks you're all marvellous, because you are,' said Sharon, hugging anyone she could reach.

'Say thanks to your mum,' said Toby to Sky when the news had finished.

'She thought it made a good story. She said you and Leroy were alright, loyal kind of kids.'

'She liked you both a lot,' added Ginger.

Toby grinned, surprised. Sky and Ginger had turned out to be alright too, he thought.

Chapter 10
First Match of the Season

'Stand still while I spray you,' said Sharon, 'blue or yellow?'

Toby wasn't sure about the hair dye but Matty caught his eye and gave him a thumbs up. Rose got them all in a line to dance to 'We are the Champions!'

She talked them through the routine,

'Kick, clap, punch.' When it came to 'We are the Champions of the World' they had to jump up as high as they could. Matty joined in, standing next to Toby.

The other team looked a bit surprised, but news of The Colts and The Mum Manager had spread. There was a rumour that the T.V. cameras might come today so there were lots of supporters crowding round. Toby noticed that people looked a bit smarter than usual, he felt a buzz of excitement.

Toby caught Leroy's eye and grinned as Lofty did an extra wiggle and waved his arms about at the end of the dance.

'Great move Lofty,' said Rose.

'That was brilliant fun,' said Matty smiling. 'Now get in your positions and good luck.'

He and Sharon stood on the sideline watching the team kick off against Parton Pumas.

The game was fast and furious. Sky played as a striker and Toby had to try to cross the ball to her. Toby tackled the number 10 and ran down the wing. He swerved round a defender, just like Matty had showed him and crossed the ball to Sky.

She took it early volleying it into the net. The Colts were 1-0 up.

'Great strike Sky!' said Sharon.

Then danger loomed as Lofty failed to deal with a pass back and the ball bobbled near the line. As he ran back to grab it Lofty collided with a defender and the two clashed heads.

Oh no, Rose is on, thought Toby, as Rose ran on to the pitch. He remembered the collision in the last match.

'OK, let's look. It's just a knock,' she said holding an ice pack on Lofty's bump. 'That should do it, carry on.' She sprinted off again.

Leroy and Toby glanced at one another and grinned. *Rose seems more efficient today*, thought Toby, *less excitable, good in fact.*

Just before half time Toby found he was unmarked. Jacko passed to him. Toby dribbled the ball down the wing and looked around for Sky. She wasn't in a good position and was hidden by a defender.

'Have a shot Toby,' she yelled.

Toby steadied himself and belted the ball. It screamed into the back of the net, in the bottom left hand corner.

'Goal!' he yelled and was mobbed by Leroy and Sky.

Sky put out her hand to give Toby a high five. He hesitated but then slapped her hand. *She's OK*, he thought, *for a girl!*

At the half time whistle the team jogged off. They were 2-0 up.

'It's going great isn't it?' said Toby to Leroy.

'I know, even Rose managed not to flatten anyone,' replied Leroy.

As Sharon passed round drinks and

orange slices, Matty put up his hand to get their attention.

'Fabulous play Colts. I'm off now. You don't need my help today. I'm happy to leave you in the capable hands of Sharon and Rose. I'll keep in touch though.'

Toby ran after him. 'Thanks.'

Matty turned and said, 'I thought it was going to be hard at first. But Sharon and Rose - they're alright. Really enthusiastic. And you Tobias, you've learned to accept Sky and to stop being embarrassed by Sharon. I think The Colts are going to be fine.'

'How do you know that?' asked Toby.

'It's all about playing to your strengths. Sharon and Rose have lots of good points.

You lot are really fit after all the dancing and the yoga. The Colts really are a team with a difference.'

Toby waved to Matty and went back to join the others. He looked at Sharon with new eyes. She was efficiently collecting drinks bottles and giving a team talk.

'Just keep on playing the same way. It's working. Play like this every week and I think you could be champions.' She looked up and winked at Toby.

I think she might just be right, thought Toby, *Three Cheers for The Mum Manager!*

Also available in the Reluctant Reader Series from:

PUBLISHING

Sam's Spitfire Summer *(WW2 Adventure)*
Ian MacDonald   ISBN 978 1 905637 43 0

Alien Teeth   *(Humorous Science Fiction)*
Ian MacDonald   ISBN 978 1 905637 32 2

Eyeball Soup   *(Science Fiction)*
Ian MacDonald   ISBN 978 1 904904 59 5

Chip McGraw   *(Cowboy Mystery)*
Ian MacDonald   ISBN 978 1 905637 08 9

Close Call   *(Mystery - Interest age 12+)*
Sandra Glover   ISBN 978 1 905 637 07 2

Beastly Things in the Barn   *(Humorous)*
Sandra Glover   ISBN 978 1 904904 96 0
www.sandraglover.co.uk

Cracking Up   *(Humorous)*
Sandra Glover   ISBN 978 1 904904 86 1

Deadline   *(Adventure)*
Sandra Glover   ISBN 978 1 904904 30 4

The Crash   *(Mystery)*
Sandra Glover   ISBN 978 1 905637 29 4

The Owlers   *(Adventure)*
Stephanie Baudet   ISBN 978 1 904904 87 8

The Curse of the Full Moon *(Mystery)*
Stephanie Baudet   ISBN 978 1 904904 11 3

A Marrow Escape *(Adventure)*
Stephanie Baudet   ISBN 1 900818 82 5

The One That Got Away *(Humorous)*
Stephanie Baudet   ISBN 1 900818 87 6

Donkeys Wings and Worm Strings *(Multicultural)*
Adam Bushnell   ISBN 978 1 905637 50 8

Trevor's Trousers *(Humorous)*
David Webb   ISBN 978 1 904904 19

The Library Ghost *(Mystery)*
David Webb   ISBN 978 1 904374 66

Dinosaur Day *(Adventure)*
David Webb   ISBN 978 1 904374 67 1

Grandma's Teeth *(Humorous)*
David Webb   ISBN 978 1 905637 20 1

Friday the Thirteenth *(Humorous)*
David Webb   ISBN 978 1 905637 37 9

The Curse of the Pharaoh's Tomb
                            (Egyptian Adventure)
David Webb   ISBN 978 1 905637 42 3

The Alien Science Bus *(Sci-fi)*
Derek Keilty   ISBN 978 1 905637 46 1

The Bears Bite Back *(Humorous)*
Derek Keilty   ISBN 978 1 905637 36 2

Order online @ **www.eprint.co.uk**